MW01035488

Liberty, Justice, & F'rall

The Dog Heroes of the Texas Republic

by

Marjorie Kutchinski

EAKIN PRESS ★ Austin, Texas

For Paul
Marjorie Kutchinski

Published in the United States of America
By Eakin Press
A Division of Sunbelt Media, Inc.
P.O. Box 90159
Austin, Texas 78709
email: eakinpub@sig.net

3 4 5 6 7 8 9

ISBN 1-57168-217-1

This is a work of fiction.

Library of Congress Cataloging-in-Publication Data

Kutchinski, Marjorie.
Liberty, Justice & F'rall: The Dog Heroes of The Texas Republic / by Marjorie Kutchinski.
p. cm.
Summary: Sam Houston's dog Liberty describes how she and Sam's other dogs, Justice and F'rall, played a key role in the history of the Texas Republic and the Battle of San Jacinto.
ISBN 1-57168-217-1
1. Houston, Sam, 1793-1863—Juvenile fiction. 2. Texas—History—Revolution, 1835-1836—Juvenile fiction. [1. Houston, Sam, 1793-1863—Fiction 2. Texas—History—Revolution, 1835-1836—Fiction. 3. Dogs—Fiction.] I. Title.
PZ7.K967Li 1998
[Fic]-dc21
97-48558
CIP AC

Dedicated to the Memory of the Texas Veteran Association

At the last meeting of the Texas Veteran Association in 1907, only six members attended. After a memorial service, each of these men expressed that due to increasing infirmities of age, he would be unable to attend another meeting. Before adjourning for the last time, it was resolved that "the holy memories clinging around it should be merged into the patriotic association, the Daughters of the Republic of Texas," founded in 1891. The old heroes then laid aside their badges and bequeathed their memories and deeds as a precious legacy to the Daughters of the Republic of Texas to be held in "trust forever."

Acknowledgment to the Author

The Daughters of the Republic of Texas acknowledge with deep gratitude the transfer of literary rights to *Liberty, Justice, and F'rall: The Dog Heroes of the Texas Republic* from author, Marjorie Kutchinski. By this gift to the DRT, and the publication of this book, her gracious act helps us continue to revere the past, present and future of "Texas, one and indivisible," and our inestimable heritage.

Mrs. Tookie Dempsey Walthall
President General 1997-1999
The Daughters of the Republic of Texas

Contents

Contents

How This Story Came To Be

The fall of the Alamo and the victory at San Jacinto made Texas a nation. These events have inspired poems, songs, books, and movies. But so far no one has told the entire story. After over 155 years, credit should go where credit is due. It is time for Liberty, Justice, and F'rall—my ancestors, the dog heroes owned by Sam Houston—to take their rightful place in history.

This story was written by Liberty, the female dog hero of the Republic. It is a true story. The original document is now at the Dogs of the Republic of Texas headquarters. It was not easy to find. However, as the oldest member of my family, I inherited the knowledge of where to find the secret document. Of course, I will never reveal where I found it on the Alamo grounds. I spent all of four nights digging. Finally, on the fifth night I found it safe and dry in a mesquite case lined with tin. My heart thumped. My paws trembled. I sat down to read the long lost account. Liberty's story was hard to read. Spelling has never been a strong point in our family, and please remember that in those days dogs received little education. But the paw mark at the end proved it was the real thing.

If you read carefully, you'll notice Liberty not only tells the story of her life with Sam Houston, but also makes a plea for humans to act more like dogs. In these troubled times, the world would be a better place if everyone followed her advice—love the most you can love, eat well, sleep when you're tired, be forgiving and loyal, use Sam's recipe for fear, do what makes you happy, and be sure you get petted every day.

LADY—
Retriever, Historian, and Chair-dog of Dogs of the Republic of Texas.

-1- Liberty Meets Sam

My earliest memory is riding in Sam Houston's pocket as he headed for Texas. I used to think I was born in that pocket, always being tossed about and covered with peanut shells, tobacco, seeds, or whatever else he dropped in on top of me. Sometimes my tail ended up in my mouth. Crumbs from a corn cob he chewed on from time to time got in my eyes and ears. Now and then the strong smell of tobacco made me sneeze and my eyes water.

Once I thought he might be a monster.

Maybe he'd eat me along with the peanuts when I got fat enough.

One day Sam held me up in both hands and looked me right in the eye. My heart raced. My muscles tensed, and my breathing got faster as I tried to slip away from him. "Liberty," he said. "You're afraid of me!"

I pushed my nose under his shirt button.

"Don't hide it. Be glad when you feel fearful. It's your alarm system. That warning might save your life someday. Take a deep breath and look at me. I'm not a bear, and I never eat puppies."

I closed my eyes and took a deep breath. When I looked at him he was laughing at me.

"You're a beautiful female pup. Your mother was the favorite dog of the president of the United States, Andrew Jackson. You are a token of his regard for me. He promised you would always keep me in line and help me find great rewards in Texas."

What a giant responsibility! I crept back into Sam's pocket—stunned, but not afraid to live up to the president's promise. What a relief to know I was a dog—especially a female dog with a noble background. After that day, bits of my early training and heritage came back to my memory whenever I needed to remember what dogs do. Sam said I left my mother too soon, but he would help me catch up fast.

A day with Sam was never dull. He was full of fun and unpredictable. His success and fame now depended on me. I was proud to take on such a noble task, but I worried about it often in those days. Keeping Sam Houston safe was my life's work. No matter what happened, he would always come first with me.

I had just about outgrown his pocket when my first test came. We were riding along through a deep, wooded area when suddenly a large deer with horns leapt in front of us. The horse spooked, reared up once, and then reared again when a wildcat raced after the deer. Sam was thrown from his horse. He landed on a ridge and rolled head over heels down a gully, then hit his head on a rock at the bottom.

The fall didn't hurt fat and furry me, but Sam landed on his back with his pocket pulled tight at the top. I was trapped. My only hope depended on a tiny hole in one corner of Sam's pocket. My claws and my teeth worked on that hole until it was big enough to squeeze through.

Sam was still out cold. It was up to me to save him.

I licked his face. I barked and nipped at his ears. I made terrible noises to wake him.

He didn't move. I licked until my tongue stopped working. Then I nudged and pushed him with my body, but he lay still as a stone.

I had a wild thought. This might be my only opportunity to bite him on the nose, I thought. In the dog world, biting another dog's nose puts the biter in control. I took a big chance in doing that, but if he was my responsibility I needed to be in command. With a man like Sam it's better not to let him know that he is being controlled. This was the perfect time. I reached up and bit him.

With that bite his hand came up to brush me away. Then I rested while patting his cheek with my paw until he finally woke up. What a relief when he told me to go away.

"It's hard to dream when a tiny furry whirlwind is charging and barking. Thanks for waking me, Chum. I'll return the favor some day." He took me in his arms and petted me. "I know what I can do to reward you," he told me.

He went on, "I ran away from home to live with the Cherokee Indians when I was still a boy. Chief Jim Jolly adopted me and raised me as his son. I left when I grew up and wanted to study law, but my heart stayed with the Indians. His camp will always be home to me. Liberty, you need to grow up there as I did. You'll learn what you need to know from the Indian dogs. We'll start right now."

We rode toward the Cherokees with me across the saddle in front of Sam. My body wasn't long enough for me to feel safe in the saddle. I would have slipped off many times if Sam's hand had not been on my back to hold me. The best part was that I got to see the countryside. Sam talked to me about the Indians. I became excited about seeing other dogs.

After a few days I got used to riding on Sam's lap, and learned to dig my claws into his britches to stay put. Sam shouted and yanked at me when my claws went through the cloth into his groin. By the time we got to the Indian camp, I had learned to hold on without scratching his skin.

"Welcome. My wigwam is yours," Chief Jim Jolly greeted Sam. His scouts had brought word we were coming, so a feast was being prepared for us.

All the Indians called Sam "Colonel" and treated him like a treasured brother. Sam said his name meant "raven." He called all the braves by their Cherokee names, and acted as if he had come home.

I was afraid to leave Sam's sight. The Indian dogs looked huge and mean, showed their teeth, and made strange noises when they came close. Sam protected me.

Sam showed me the special Indian ways and prepared me to live as he did. He wore a beaded doeskin shirt, leather leggings, and a feather headdress. He let his hair and beard grow long, and he spoke Cherokee every day.

He said the words over and over to me until I understood them.

As I grew bigger, I learned to hunt rabbits, squirrels, and turkeys with the Indian dogs. Old He-dog became a good friend and helped me learn to get along with the others. He stared at them eye to eye, daring them to bother me. Soon they treated me as if I belonged. Run-with-Wind shared her skill for finding eggs. Sam hugged me and hooted the day I brought him a fresh prairie chicken egg in my mouth without breaking it. Elk-dog showed me how to find deer. They all taught me how to act like a rock when we hunted, and how to run without making any noise.

Many times I showed Sam where to find deer when the tribe needed food. He called me a rare hunter. He whispered in my ear that I had become even better than the Indian dogs.

"You can outsmell, outsee, and outhear

any animal or man I've ever known. You can run for hours without stopping. You can swim any river. You're not afraid to help me do anything I want to do, and you are beautiful, Liberty."

I'll admit my long, silky, light brown fur wasn't like any of the scrawny Indian dogs'. Plus I was a head taller than most of them. But Sam looked at me with his heart. He saw only my best side, and he didn't always tell the truth. I also thought Sam was beautiful. The Indian dogs told me Sam was the ugliest man they ever saw.

He liked to run his hands through my fur when he had a problem to think about. Petting me helped him feel calm, and I made sure he remembered to do it often. That was part of my training of Sam. But it didn't take long for me to realize that biting Sam's nose gave me no control over him at all. That was when I made up my mind to find him a wife just as soon as we made it to Texas. He needed more help than I could give him, and he enjoyed ladies.

But poor Sam never learned to appreciate outstanding smells. On the best day of my life, He-dog and Elk-dog showed me where to find fresh elk dung. We rolled in it back and forth, front and rear, we barked and frolicked around in it. I'd never known such a marvelous smell. Nothing ever felt better. We were the happiest of dogs until we reached camp. When we came near our tepee, Sam held his nose and ordered me to the river. He chased me away whenever I came near. Even the Indians avoided us.

We three dogs sulked around in the dark on the edge of camp—outcasts. What a disappointment to learn humans didn't appreciate elk dung. I'd never slept away from Sam before, and wondered how he got along without me.

Sam encouraged the Indians to stop fighting each other and band together. Some agents of the government were robbing and cheating them.

Sam sat cross-legged, using a book and my back as a desk to write President Jackson about it. When he did this, he expected me to act like a tree. If I moved a hair, he shouted at me.

"Hold still, Liberty! How do you expect me to write with you scratching and thumping your tail?"

When he finished the letter, he sat back and sighed. "I've found the perfect place to be. My people need me, and I like living here," Sam said, grinning from ear to ear.

I thought we'd live there forever, and that he had forgotten all about Texas.

But one day Sam and I were resting on the bank of the Tennessee river, my head in his lap, when an eagle swooped down low over the water. It nearly touched us, gave a mighty cry, rose up and flew toward the west.

Sam jumped to his feet. “That’s my talisman,” he shouted. “Come on, Liberty, we’re leaving for Texas.”

-2- Love Comes and Goes

We made a sad parting with our Indian family. Sam sulked for days on the trail. I ran in circles after my tail, jumped out of a bush at him, yelped like a coyote, but nothing I did cheered him or made him laugh.

"Shut up, Liberty," he bellowed at me, and remained glum and moody. I even avoided elk dung, and smiled a lot, but his dark mood remained.

I always knew what Sam was thinking. When one eyebrow went up, I stayed close to protect him. When he searched the sky, I howled and pawed the ground, ready to strike terror into the heart of an enemy. When his tongue pushed at his cheek, I ran ahead to see what was coming.

Sam was a strange, complicated person with a temper like a volcano, yet I always knew what to expect of him. When he roared at me with special anger in his voice, I ran for cover. Once he took the wrong trail and blamed me, "Keep your eyes open, Liberty. You missed the turnoff." I barked back at him until he sat down in the saddle, covered his ears with his big hands, and let me lead him to the right trail. Sometimes he ignored my barks. Then I'd find a place to hide and cover my ears with my paws until he apologized.

We were both surprised one day. We had nearly reached the Red River and were excited about going into Texas territory at last when someone rode toward us through a thicket. "Sam!" yelled a raw-boned, giant of a man. He jumped off his horse and pulled

Sam to the ground beside him. They slapped each other on the back several times and laughed like school boys.

"You still ride alligators and lasso deer, Bowie? You tough old rough hide!"

"No. I moved to Texas. I invented the best knife in the world and named it after me. We're both famous." Bowie strutted about and showed off his knife by throwing it into a tree He offered it to Sam. Sam threw it and grinned when it hit his mark.

They talked without stopping the rest of the day and most of the night. I stopped listening to them. You might say I was distracted. Walking beside Jim Bowie's horse was the most magnificent male dog I had ever seen. His short black fur was thick and glossy down to his white paws. Bowie called him Justice. Justice skidded to a stop in front of me and stared. His eyes shone. I dropped to my elbows, ready for a romp. He chased me around the camp site. We circled trees, bounced over brush, frightened birds, woke up two deer in the woods, and jumped streams. Our paws seldom touched the ground. With shining eyes and bursting energy we frolicked about, racing close to the men and back again, nearly knocking Sam to the ground. He shouted at us to go away.

We never got tired. Before the sun went down, we had raced though the brush to the river twice, and chased four rabbits and a beaver. I brought Sam a big, fat rabbit. Justice caught a fish in the stream and brought it to Bowie. His splendid body moved as fast as a deer.

Love filled me with awe and wonder. I knew I'd found my mate.

We ate and slept with our fur touching each other. When Justice came near, I buried my head in his mantle. I hoped we would be together forever, but we parted the next morning. I wanted to go with him, but my life's work was with Sam. I knew I would never love another.

"Justice is a marvelous beast. I traded a sheep for him from a German farmer. Best deal I ever made, but he understands commands in German. I had to learn them fast. But as long as I live, I'll never be without Justice. He is everything I ever hoped for in a dog—part human, if you know what I mean," Bowie told Sam.

Sam laughed and patted Justice's thick coat. He put his hand over his handsome, cold nose.

"Every man needs a good dog, Bowie. We are both blessed."

My heart felt like breaking as we parted. I whined and howled. Justice moaned. He wanted to come with us, but he had pledged his loyalty to Bowie.

Sam cheered me some by saying, "You'll see him again, Liberty." I knew I must.

"Nacogdoches is the place for you to go, Sam. They don't have a lawyer, and they need a good man like you to help the settlers get a fair deal when they buy land. You'll fit in just fine. Just don't forget Texas belongs to Mexico. You do what they say. You're not in the United States here. Things are different."

Sam lost no time in taking Bowie's advice. I sulked along behind him, wishing I could follow Justice who went in the opposite direction, but not for long. I had to stay alert on the trail because Sam liked to read his book while he rode along. He counted on my barks to tell him when he needed to stop reading.

One day I warned him about a coiled rattlesnake in our path. He had time to turn the horse off the trail and avoid it. Armadillos were another problem. Sam's horse hated them. He spooked every time he saw one. I developed a special bark for armadillos to let Sam know he was getting close to one. Unfortunately, the horse never learned what my barks meant, and I had to be responsible for both of them.

After Sam swam his horse across the Red River and rode into Texas, his spirits rose. He smiled, laughed, and played with me more often, but never stopped during the day for me to nap. There are limits to my good nature, and that trip drained my strength. No naps, and hardly any time to scratch or roll or chase rabbits, seemed like no life at all.

One day I'd had enough. I stopped in the middle of the trail, stretched out, and closed my eyes. I would have stayed there forever and let Sam go on alone, but he also stopped. He found a small pond of clear water nearby. He let the horse graze and took off his clothes for a swim.

"Watch my clothes!" he shouted as he jumped in.

When I finished that needed nap, Sam found a low tree on the other side of the pond. He held on to it, bobbed up and down in the water, and shouted to me. I heard him saying something about clothes, so I gathered them in my mouth and swam out to him.

"Stop!" Sam bellowed at me.

I turned around, swam back to the shore, dropped his wet clothes, and ran to hide under a bush.

"Dumb dog! You stupid dog," he shouted as he pulled himself out of the water and ran toward me. "You come here and take your punishment. Bad dog!"

I was smart enough not to let him find me, but I watched him from a safe place. He spent a long time yanking his leather leggings and shirt onto his wet body.

After he finally managed to get dressed,

he hunted for me. He beat the bushes with a long stick and called my name.

I left the safety of my hiding place after he mounted and rode back on the trail. I stayed far behind. He didn't see me until he stopped for the night. By then he was dry, but he was still angry at me. I curled up in a hollow spot and went to sleep. I knew Sam would never hurt me because he had a weakness for a wet nose and adoring glances, but I was embarrassed.

We traveled through forests for days and then came to the plains covered with grass and low brush. We saw a herd of wild cattle and circled around them, but we ate well on the turkeys and rabbits I hunted on the trail. Sam became more thoughtful of me and stopped for a nap when I hung my head close to the ground and moaned. He stretched out on the ground, and used his hat for a pillow. I curled up on a grassy spot near him.

Sam found a small cabin in Nacogdoches soon after we arrived. It was an ugly town with tiny adobe huts and unpaved streets. I hoped we'd move back into the wilderness because I missed the critters there. Sam told me I'd find plenty of critters in offices.

"This place has great promise. You'll get used to it, Liberty," Sam told me.

I did, but not until I'd lost blood and some fur on my neck fighting to win my status as the most important dog on our street. No dog questioned my rank, but a large black cat refused to give me the respect I deserved. She was a stuck-up cat from Boston, built like an overloaded wagon. She had to be watched at all times.

I also learned the advantages of a warm bed, food on demand, and the luxury of the cabin.

Sam put away his Indian clothes, cut his hair, and shaved his beard. He even joined the Catholic church, as he was required to do. He began to help people buy and sell land.

It was hard for me to adjust to his new ways and live in a town. Being in the wilds suited me. Sam expected me to stay at his feet when he worked so I could turn away men he didn't want to see. With a special look from him I snarled; I barked and bristled; I foamed at the mouth like a savage. I wished I could teach Sam to bite, to go with his sharp tongue and quick fist.

Sam got along well with most of the people around Nacogdoches and never tired of being with them day and night. They talked and laughed all night long—exciting stuff if you could stay awake. Sam resented my barking and snapping at his boots when I thought it was time to leave a party.

"Liberty, you are not my mother. I'm happy here. I'll go home when I please. Sit down and shut up."

I would turn around in a tight circle and land in the perfect spot near his foot—unless there was a kitchen. I liked the talk better there, and could help out by eating up the leftovers and listening to the gossip.

We both became smarter by being good listeners and watching. I've found that good manners and a soulful expression will get you anywhere. Sam needed to work on a soulful expression and stop wearing out his boots on a brass rail.

When he wrote letters, I always sat at his feet and listened. He spoke aloud as he wrote. His letters to President Jackson and other friends in the East all sounded the same: "I may make Texas my home. Desperadoes, gamblers, and adventurers have drifted in from the states as well as Europe. I've learned how to handle them and keep the peace. The shopkeepers and farmers are my best friends. Everyone who stays is supposed to be a Mexican citizen, but for every six rough foreigners, there is only one Mexican. I know of no man who wants to be controlled by the Mexican government. One day these homesteaders will all get together and do something about that."

I listened to Sam talk about the coming trouble as he tried to understand and help the people who had settled in Texas. Sometimes he had to show them how to behave. It made me proud to know that he never allowed anyone in his sight to beat a dog, a horse, or a child. "Animals and children never forget a lesson in meanness," he often told me.

I spent my time roaming the countryside, following trails, and learning where Sam's enemies lived. I watched for wolves, deer, and, most importantly, unmarried ladies who knew how to cook.

"War is coming soon, Liberty," he told me

one day. “Texas settlers want to control what happens here.”

I wondered what would be expected of me. I worried because I knew I’d soon have pups to raise.

-3-
How to Grow a Prince of a Pup

Sam won the hearts of the people in Nacogdoches. He made male friends with a handshake, and most ladies made a fuss over him. They laughed with him as they followed him about. I tried to keep some of them away, but Sam liked them all.

His middle name should have been "whittle." He did his best work carving baskets out of peach stones for pretty young ladies of his choice. I hoped to find a girl who cooked well to marry him. None of them lived up to my standards.

His fame grew fast all over Texas. He was

a gifted speaker. He spoke to anyone who would listen to him, anywhere, and for any reason. Sam told me he had been governor of Tennessee, so telling people what they should do was what he did best. He was a lot like me. Charm gets you more than yelping or barking ever will. We were both smart and natural leaders, and he talked enough for both of us. Lucky me, I didn't have to listen when he spoke. I learned to look interested in what he said with my eyes shut, unless food was served. Then I'd sit near clumsy eaters who always dropped a share for me on the floor.

The frontier suited him as it did me. We were both busy because soon after we settled in our cabin my litter of one arrived.

"Liberty, and Justice . . . F'rall," Sam shouted when he saw my pup. "His name must be F'rall!"

I had expected more than just one, but F'rall had all the best traits of ten pups. He bounced around like a good rubber ball, curious about everything. He made humanlike sounds between barks, and he hummed in his sleep. Sam predicted he'd be a talker and that he would learn fast.

Many different languages were spoken in Nacogdoches. Sam said we must understand all the greetings. He hoped to teach F'rall to say them in English, Spanish, Italian, French, and German. Sam said the words over and over every day. Soon F'rall put his head in the air, and moved his mouth around until strange noises rattled around in his throat. When the sounds came close to the word, Sam hooted, hugged F'rall, and gave him a piece of jerky.

Sam practiced words with him too much. F'rall should have been outside chasing rabbits or deer, and learning to dig. There was only one way to stop Sam from overtraining him. I'd jump into the horse watering trough, come back inside and shower Sam with my shakes. While he bellowed at me to stop, I'd run away with F'rall. We'd race into the woods where I could teach him the important things the Indian dogs had taught me. He learned dog skills fast. Sam bragged that he could almost say "hello" in four languages before he was grown, even if he only moaned the German greeting. Sam could never pronounce it correctly either.

Sam sat in his big rocker with F'rall on his lap, coaching him for hours at a time. He spoiled him for sure. My little darling thought he was a lap dog.

That became a problem. He grew big fast. His head was soon higher than Sam's when he jumped onto his lap. Sam tried to break him of the habit by pushing him off and shouting at him. He stayed away while Sam was awake. It was another story when Sam took a nap in his chair. F'rall would walk up to the chair slowly, one paw at a time. Then he'd turn around and push his rear end up the sleeping man's legs until he almost stood on his nose. Then he'd ease himself onto Sam's lap. He'd sit there smiling until Sam woke up and heaved him across the room. F'rall waited for his next nap to try again.

Much as I loved F'rall, I had to admit he grew up ugly. He got none of Justice's good looks and not an ounce of my beauty. He had an ugly mouse-colored coat with spots of brown and black here and there. It was thick and wiry as a stiff brush. One ear stood up and the other flopped half down. He had little pig eyes, but a smile any mother could rave about. When he smiled his face became relaxed, with his ears low, eyes half shut, lips parted, and chin high. Even with that lovely smile, Sam called him half wolf and half donkey.

F'rall learned early how to make Sam

laugh. When Sam pretended to shoot him and shouted "bang," he dropped dead and stayed there with his legs held high and stiff until Sam told him to get up. Sometimes Sam placed food on F'rall's nose. The pup held it there until Sam gave the signal to toss it in the air and catch it in his mouth.

By the time he was a year old, Sam bragged to his friends that he'd taught F'rall ten tricks.

"He can outsee, outhear, outsmell, outswim, and outrun any living thing except you, Liberty. He is a natural herder. If you didn't look at his face, you'd say he was the smartest pup in Texas."

Sam was right. F'rall herded everything in sight. When our neighbor's chickens went too far away from her house, he brought them back. One day he found the same lady's four little children down by the river and herded them home. They didn't want to go with him.

They screamed and cried all the way. The children's mother chased F'rall away with a stick. She shouted and tried to hit him again and again, crying, "I sent those children to the river to find their father. You go away and leave my children alone!"

F'rall came to Sam with his tail between his legs and a sad face. Sam petted him and said, "You're the world's best herder. You keep right on doing what you do best. The time will come when you'll make us proud."

One day Sam sat at his desk writing a letter. F'rall rounded up a goat, two sheep, and a goose and brought them into the cabin. Sam didn't look up until the goose nipped his arm and the goat had eaten the brim off his hat. F'rall had stretched himself across the doorway. Sam laughed and hooted at first. There was no holding that dog back when he had the urge to herd. When the sheep made a mess on the floor, Sam ordered them all out at once, and F'rall took over. All but the goose left. She was chewing on one of Sam's books and refused to leave. F'rall had to grab her tail feathers in his teeth to get her attention. She bit his ear. He whimpered all the time he snapped at her, in order to push her out of the cabin.

"No herding inside!" Sam shouted.

But most of the time he encouraged F'rall to do what made him happy.

"Some of Justice's kin must have been outstanding herders," Sam said. "His gift might came in handy someday, especially when the fighting starts."

Sam tried to teach us both to run and hide when we heard a shot. We refused to do that. If danger came, I wanted to be there to take care of him. F'rall lay down with his paws over his ears when he heard a shot, but I knew he would always be there to help me protect Sam.

F'rall and I heard about the trouble in the

town of Gonzales before Sam did. We were chasing each other around a mesquite tree a good run from town, when a man on horseback came galloping toward us. He pulled up to shout to a farmer nearby.

"Fighting's started! Texans are whipping the Mexicans in Gonzales."

We raced back to town to find people shouting and dancing in the street. Everybody in Nacogdoches seemed to be celebrating. People shouted, "Texans drove the Mexicans out of San Antonio!"

We found Sam in the crowd listening to the messenger on horseback. Sam looked worried. He stood on a tree stump and talked to the people.

"Now those settlers will think they are brave and bold enough to do anything. They have no training, and they all think the war is over and it's time to go home. The men who stay will want to be generals," Sam warned.

"They were foolish to fight before they were prepared. I've fought in a war. I know." Many crowded around Sam as he talked on and on about being prepared.

The next day as we escorted Sam to town, another messenger arrived. He jumped from his horse and talked to anyone who would listen.

"I've just come by boat from Brownsville to Indianola. A man loaned me this horse to spread the bad news. Before I left Brownsville I saw Santa Anna, the president and general of Mexico, cross the Rio Grande. He's marching his troops toward San Antonio. He plans to put down the Texans for good! Prepare!"

The people of Nacogdoches crowded around Sam, asking him what they should do. He was full of ideas, and they listened to him. F'rall and I napped and kept the rabbits away.

The next day several men came to the cabin to tell Sam he had been elected by the citizens of Texas to command the Texas forces. Sam seemed happy when he heard the news. He was ready to take over, and it sounded like our "doing nothing" days were over. F'rall got excited. I crawled under the bed for a nap.

He sold his land on the Red River in order to have a magnificent general's uniform made. It had lots of stars. A flaming red sash secured a sword to his waist. He liked to put it on and strut around. When he wore it, F'rall and I rolled on the floor and waved our paws in the air. We put our noses on his boots to show respect, and learned to bark with rapture when he appeared.

We knew Sam could do anything he wanted to do, and so did he. The first thing he did as general was to send out dozens of messengers to ask for volunteers to come and fight for Texas. Sam sent them away with these orders: "Tell everyone you meet. Volunteers can earn land by fighting, but they need to bring their own guns and ammunition. Tell them they are needed at once!"

Every day he sent out more couriers to spread the news. He even sent a man to New Orleans to advertise in the newspaper.

But most of the time he sat at his desk writing to settlers, telling them how to prepare for war.

"Soon men will come from all over Texas and the eastern and southern states. We will meet the volunteers in Gonzales," Sam said. "Liberty and F'rall, rest and eat well. I'll need help."

-4-
Wet Dogs Are Welcomed

Texas winter weather often changed from hot to cold in a few minutes without any warning. One hot winter day F'rall and I were napping in the dirt near the cabin during the heat of the day. I was in the middle of my second nap when F'rall's chattering teeth woke me. We huddled together as the brisk wind blew my fur away from my body. The air smelled like dust and seemed to get colder with every blast.

After a while the wind stopped. Then a light snow fell all around us. We jumped up and leapt into the air trying to catch the falling snow. Snow was new to F'rall. We danced around the yard, mouths wide, snapping at the flakes. Sam came out of the cabin to get a log. We followed him back inside. He rubbed us down with an old sack and left us to dry near the fireplace. Then he picked up a letter he had just written.

"This is to Jim Bowie. You'll want to hear it, Liberty."

Just then a pesky flea pierced my rear and sent me into a twisted frenzy to scratch it. Sam hit me twice with the letter to get my attention. I suffered the terrible itch and listened.

"Dear Jim," he read. "As a colonel of the Texas militia, I order you to San Antonio to take joint command of the Alamo with William Barret Travis. As soon as you arrive, destroy the Alamo and everything in it. We don't have the horses and wagons needed to remove the cannons. Destroy them so the Mexicans can't use them against us. Do it at once! Santa Anna is marching toward San Antonio. Sam Houston, Commanding General."

"Liberty, now you know where to find Justice," Sam sighed.

I hoped Justice would be safe in San Antonio. I worried about us, too. A messenger arrived with news that the Indians were fighting settlers.

"I must go talk with the tribe at once," Sam said as he pulled out his Indian clothes. "You come with me," he told us.

We got his horse ready, and we all left that afternoon. He rode toward East Texas to try to make peace before more trouble started.

"Maybe if I explain to them how much we need them they'll help us fight the Mexicans. We can't fight both of them," he said over and over again. We were too cold to listen. We hoped he would find the camp before we froze.

We huddled together that night on the trail, too cold to sleep. Sam shivered and tossed until the sky cleared and a full moon appeared. He had us back on the trail the rest of the night. The next day the sun shone to warm and dry us. We stopped and slept in the sun until Sam called us to wake up and move on. I decided we needed food before the trip, so I killed a fat rabbit. Sam cooked it, and we shared it before we left our camp.

"I'll pacify those Indians, make peace, and talk them into fighting with the Texans against the Mexicans," Sam said. He practiced speaking Cherokee for his speech to the chief.

"We may need the Indians to win against Santa Anna!" Sam announced.

Two days later we found the tribe. They were thin and hungry. The chief told Sam that food had been scarce in the camp all winter. The adults saved most of the food for the children, but they also looked starved and gaunt.

The Indians depended on dried buffalo meat in the winter months. But the settlers had been shooting buffalo to make robes, not food. They wasted the meat. All the other animals they hunted had gone south for the winter. The desperate Indians were forced to raid the settlers for food. Sam's eyes filled with tears when he heard the Indians' sad tale.

My custom was to stay near Sam, but F'rall liked to run off on his own. One day he disappeared, and was gone for a couple of days. On the third day I started looking for his scent, trying to find out which way he had gone.

Suddenly, I heard hooves tromping along the trail. I listened, but saw nothing. I sat down and waited. After a while a small herd of wild cattle came into view. F'rall barked them into the center of camp. He stopped beside Sam and wagged his tail and smiled.

The Indians took care of the beef, and then danced to celebrate. F'rall became the hero of the day. He was given food and more bones than he could chew in a month. He shared them with me.

Sam gave the chief many reasons why the Indians should help the Texans. However, the chief was not convinced.

"We will not fight with the Texans, but we will not fight against them," the chief assured Sam.

Sam was disappointed, but he still had hope that the Indians would help the Texans one day.

Sam's aide arrived one afternoon to tell him that an army of volunteers waited for him in Gonzales. He also brought a letter from Bowie in San Antonio. Sam turned red with anger as he read the letter.

"Bowie refused to destroy the Alamo! They think they can defend it against the

Mexicans. He promised to fire a cannon so I'll know when the battle is over." Sam put his hands on his head and moaned.

We left the Indians in peace and took the fastest trail to Gonzales.

-5-
The War Begins

"Will this rain never stop? We don't need all this mud," Sam shouted. The sky had turned black, and rain poured down a few hours after we left the Indian camp. Before long the deer trail we followed was flooded. F'rall and I got tired of splashing in deep water, but we didn't complain. Sam complained about it often. The blanket he wrapped around him dripped rain and mud. His horse looked as miserable as he did.

The rain never stopped, and we couldn't hunt game to eat. Each day our spirits dropped to a lower point, until we were exhausted and weak with hunger.

I'd given up hope of ever seeing shelter again, when I caught a whiff of wood smoke. We came to the top of a small hill and looked down on a cabin and a barn. People were living there, and they were cooking something.

Sam rode up to the cabin, splashing water and mud all over me in his haste. A tall woman and short man met him at the door. They welcomed him inside.

A few minutes later the door opened again and the woman stood in the doorway watching us sniff the tantalizing cooking smells coming from her stove.

She smiled, and F'rall responded by putting out his paw. She bent down and shook it. He looked her in the eye and grinned his best grin.

"Howdy, I'm Nellie Black, and my man is Henry," she laughed. She then motioned for us to join Sam, who was peeling off his wet clothes by the fire.

"Your visitors are called Liberty and F'rall. We all thank you. A fire has never been more welcome," Sam said.

Henry went out to take Sam's horse to the barn and returned with a sack. He rubbed us both with it, but he fussed over F'rall for a long time. My pup really oozes charm when he wants to. They didn't have a chance. Nellie fixed a bowl of scraps, and we bolted them down in ravenous gulps.

"You're starving!" she said as she took the bowl and filled it with bread and milk. It was gone almost before it reached the floor.

Sam sat at the table wrapped in two of Mrs. Black's worn blankets. He ate everything in sight while his clothes dried by the fire. Nellie Black filled our bowl once with beans and twice with milk and bread. Our appetites were bottomless. We both hate milk and bread, but we never let her know. We devoured it all with the same relish we ate the chicken scraps and gravy she gave us later. Feeling full and safe, we stretched out near the fire and fell into a deep sleep.

When we were dry, we followed Henry to the barn. He piled fresh hay to the corner for us, filled a pan with water, and petted and talked with his new friend F'rall before he shut the door. F'rall was getting more like Sam every day. I lay quietly in the darkness beside this charmer and enjoyed the best rest I'd had in days.

We spent two nights in dry comfort, full of Nellie's cooking and happy. The rain stopped when Sam called us to leave. The sun showed partly through the clouds. We left Nellie and Henry with tears in their eyes as we started our journey into a land of deep mud. The going was slow, but it didn't rain again until we arrived in Gonzales.

Gonzales was a busy place, with houses, churches, markets. A motley band of ragged, rough men were waiting for Sam to make them into an army.

At sunrise on our first morning in Gonzales, Sam had his ear close to the muddy ground, waiting as he had for two weeks for a signal from Bowie and Travis. They had promised to fire a cannon at dawn if they still held the Alamo. Sam went on kneeling in the water for a long time. The Indians had taught him well. In the past, he had been able to hear running buffalo, the tramp of horses, and the sound of gunfire many miles away. That day he heard nothing.

There was no blast to quiver the ground. Only the sound of rain broke the silence. Sam, nervous and jumpy, sloshed about in the mud like a crazy man. I heard him send a runner to Goliad, asking General Fannin to join him at once with his 400 men.

Sam confided in me that night, "What a difference it will make if those trained soldiers come to help us. We only have raw volunteers here. They don't like to take orders from anyone and have no training. They've never marched in a line. They will run away if they don't like what I tell them to do. But they have well-oiled rifles and Bowie knives. It will take all I've got to teach them to be soldiers."

We watched him try to teach them to march, to start on the left foot, to form a line, and to advance by quick step. F'rall and I learned to do that the first day.

If men behaved like dogs, Sam could bite them on the nose and they would obey him forever. With men it wasn't so easy.

"How can I turn rough independent men, who hate to drill and follow orders, into soldiers?" Sam shook his head and wondered.

I tried barking and chewing on their shoes when they turned in the wrong direction, but that didn't help. They were not in the mood to drill in the rain. They kicked at me and went on walking as they pleased.

F'rall knew what to do when we caught three men sneaking away one night. He motioned with his eyes for me to help him. He jumped on two of the runaway soldiers as they stopped to drink, while I hit the third one. We knocked their guns to the ground. F'rall showed the length of his teeth as he snarled and bristled and herded them back to Sam. One man became so angry he pulled a knife and almost threw it at F'rall. Sam saved him just in time. After that Sam put out an order: "Any man caught deserting, or hurting my dogs will hang." Even then we had to be on our guard at all times. We found out fast that war was ugly.

F'rall saw the soldiers as unruly and badly in need of discipline and shepherding. But unless they acted angry and willful, he showed respect for them. He walked beside them fearlessly with ears, head, and tail high, looking straight ahead.

Sometimes the men pretended to sneak away to see what he'd do. He would raced after them and grab one of their boots until Sam told him to let it go.

The men laughed and teased us. They treated us like we were not important. F'rall and I stopped helping with the training. We went back to napping and protecting Sam from rabbits and other critters.

One day we had been on a long run in the countryside. We were panting and short of breath as we lay down under an oak tree. The tree stood on a little knoll near the edge of town. It sheltered us somewhat from the light rain and gave a fine view of the trail. We curled up for a good rest, but we never stopped watching. Watching was what we did best.

Sam could never have just sat and

watched like we did. He got bored easily. He always kept a knife ready to whittle when he had to sit still. Unlike Sam, we felt happy and at peace doing nothing. We liked to be quiet and think. It kept our lives well-ordered. I should have taught Sam to do that.

The rain had nearly stopped. We were still resting under the tree, when a woman rode up on a horse carrying a baby in her arms. Her hair and clothes dripped with rain. The tall black man walking behind her was just as wet, and so was a large black dog limping along behind him.

The dog stopped in his tracks and stared as I did, but only for a second. I gave a frenzied bark and plunged down the slope. The black dog ran toward me, bounding like a mad thing. I nearly went out of my mind with excitement.

He was alive! Justice was alive! I covered him with frantic licking, nearly knocking him over. I leapt all around him, yelping and struggling for breath. I buried my head in his soggy fur. He licked my ear. His leg showed an open wound, and his ribs stuck out from his filthy, bruised body. He looked like he'd been hit on the shoulders and legs many times. He needed more care than I could give him. We took him to Sam, who was in town whittling a whistle for small boy.

Sam sent a soldier for food and medicine at once. He fed Justice from his hand. He rubbed him dry with a towel, and covered his wound with a healing paste. When Sam finished, Justice crept under a bush to rest. I curled up beside him while he slept.

Soon the woman with her child rode up and stopped her horse in the middle of town. She screamed a message: "I'm Susanna Dickinson. This is my daughter, Angelina. We've come from the Alamo." A crowd gath-

ered around her. The soldiers stopped marching and rushed close to hear her as well.

Sam turned gray. I could see he was heartsick when he heard Susanna cry out her news: "Santa Anna gave me this horse to bring word that he had killed everyone at the Alamo except a few women and children. He promises the same treatment to all those who opposed him. He did terrible things. Our men were so brave, and he slaughtered them." Susanna sobbed and tears ran down her cheeks. "One of the dead heroes was my husband."

As two men helped her from her horse and started to carry her into a house nearby, she stopped, stood up, and shouted at the crowd again.

"Santa Anna is heading for Gonzales! Prepare! There is no time to waste."

The men carried her and her child inside.

They gave them dry clothes and a place to rest.

"Spread the news! Everyone must prepare to leave Gonzales at once!" Sam ordered. "We have four supply wagons. Three of them can be used to carry food for the journey."

The settlers ran to their homes to pack what they needed to take with them. They rang the church bell to alert anyone who had not heard the news. Shouting and crying filled the air. The streets soon became crowded with running men and loose animals.

Sam gave orders to try and ease the confusion, but things were so hectic only a few heard him. F'rall and I stayed near Justice to protect him while he slept. After awhile we were ready to do our part.

Sam and our neighbors needed us. I was relieved that Justice seemed to feel well enough to help also.

-6-
F'rall Finds a Remedy

Sam stood near the town square staring at a cannon. "What can we do with this gun? We can't leave it for the Mexicans to use on us, and it's too heavy to be dragged through the mud. What will we do without a wagon to carry it?" Sam threw up his hands, but he soon laughed and slapped his knee when he turned around to see F'rall herding two large, unhappy mules toward him.

He shouted for soldiers to bring harnesses and long, strong ropes. Before long the reluctant mules were tied to the cannon.

Justice, F'rall, and I barked and snapped

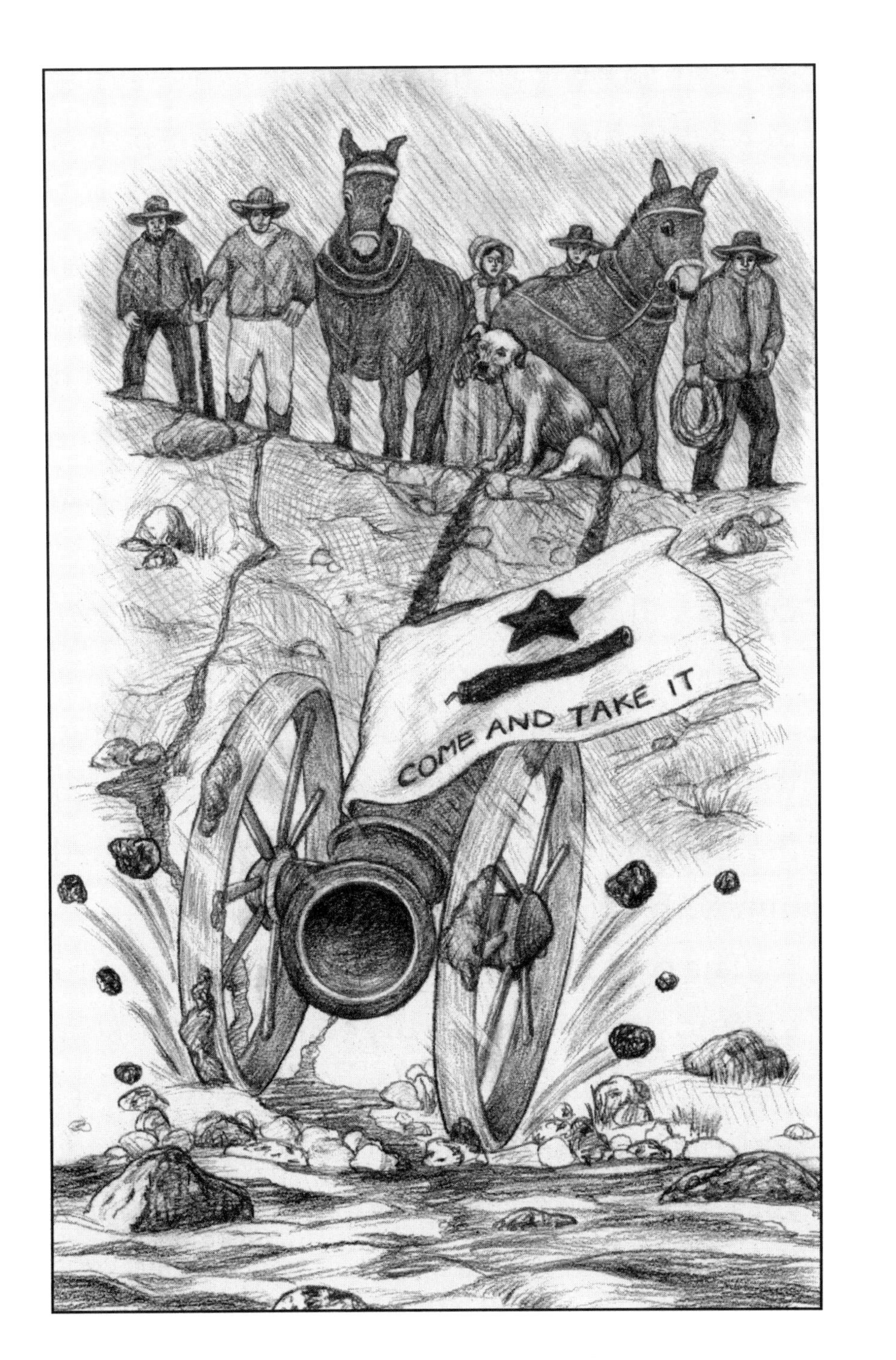
COME AND TAKE IT

at their hooves until the mules strained to move the big gun forward. Two men pulled the ropes tied to the cannon's side. Five soldiers pushed it from behind until the cannon moved through the mud to the bank of the river. Sam cut the ropes and we all watched it slide into the rain-swollen Guadalupe. The rain started pouring down again as we watched the foaming stream swallow the cannon. F'rall jumped in after it.

Soon he crawled out of the churning water and onto the bank. He sat there mumbling. We knew then that the cannon was hidden in the best place. Sam petted him and rubbed him with his wet blanket.

The colonists began a mad flight eastward to find safety. Sam urged them to stay together. F'rall herded the cows, goats, sheep, and pigs together while the people packed. Justice and I carried bundles in our teeth to the wagons and carts. He still limped yet never complained about his wounds. We worked until the carts were overflowing.

All the townspeople left their homes and fled east as fast as they could go. When they were well away from their dwellings, someone lit a barn on fire. They looked back to see nothing but smoke. Many moaned and wept as the flames turned Gonzales into ashes. They hurried on and were soon pelted by rain.

"We have nothing to come back to!" their cries filled the air.

Sam led the troops through the mud. The men staggered more than marched, sometimes slipping and pulling others down with them. Sam moved about in an old black dress coat. It was threadbare and rain soaked. Some scoundrel had stolen his blanket.

It was hard to march an army when the roads were cluttered with buggies, carts, wagons, horseback riders, and men and women walking with their livestock. Creek and river crossings were blocked by stalled wagons and carts. The army often halted to aid the travelers.

More men arrived every day to join the troops marching in the rain, but they soon complained with the others.

Later Sam said, "My army gets bigger all the time, but the new men are poorly equipped. They're hot for a fight, but they're not ready."

I was sitting on Sam's foot trying to get him to rest instead of talk about his problems. Suddenly, a runner he had sent to Goliad rushed in. "General Houston," he shouted, "Fannin and his men were captured by the Mexicans. They were all lined up and shot as traitors! First it was the Alamo and now Goliad! The Mexicans vowed to kill everybody who opposes them."

Sam was stunned. Gloom spread like a

thick fog over the men.

He felt even worse the next morning. “I lost half my troops when they heard the news, Liberty. They ran off in the night.” Sam held his head in his hands and moaned.

I felt that we three dogs should have stopped them. We all felt guilty. After that we took turns sleeping. One of us needed to watch the troops at all times, even if Sam didn't blame us for the deserters. He shouldered the responsibility himself: “The independence of Texas is now up to me. I must not make a single mistake. We will retreat until the time is right. We must not fail!”

More bad news came to him that afternoon. Indians were making war on the refugees as they rushed east in panic. The poor people didn't know where to go or what to do.

Sam sat on a stump whittling and wondering what he should do about the refugees.

F'rall stretched over his feet to keep them warm, and I pushed my nose into the palm of his hand.

"What shall I do?" he asked again and again. We stayed close to him, ready to help when he thought of a way to use us.

-7-
The Plot Thickens

I worried about Sam. He wore his Indian clothes all the time now. He even began wearing his moccasins since his only boots had given out. He went days without eating or sleeping. When he did sleep, he had only his saddle blanket and us for warmth. Justice and I pushed close by each side of him, and F'rall kept his feet warm. He seldom stopped for long, yet he never forgot our need to be petted and cared for.

His saddle bags held ears of raw corn that he gnawed at from time to time. But Sam also carried a magic formula—a small bottle of spirits of ammonia that he often sniffed. He had put shavings of deer horns in it to ward off colds. It worked for him.

He kept us almost as busy as he was. Yet, in spite of all the work, we took better care of ourselves than ever. We always found time to nap and eat. Justice and F'rall acted as scouts. I joined them when Sam didn't need me near him. Rubbing my head relaxed him and helped him think.

Sam decided the best thing to do was retreat. The troops hated retreating, but Sam had his reasons for doing it.

"We need to draw Santa Anna deeper inland," he told me. "I know the men all want to turn, find the Mexicans, and fight. They must not fight until they are ready and the time is right."

I watched them grow anxious. Many of them called Sam a coward. I growled and snarled when they said bad things about him, but that didn't stop them.

They also hated training every day. They never stopped grumbling about marching for no reason. They wanted to fight. I heard a few men whisper about sending Sam home and finding a real fighter to be general.

Sam knew what was best for them, but the troops didn't appreciate his wisdom. He needed to do something quick before they all left him.

He ordered his army to stand in parade formation, and mounted his big white stallion, Saracen. He made a stirring sight, even in his ragged clothes, hat pulled down to his ears, and covered with a wet saddle blanket.

"We can't afford to make even one mistake," he told them. "We'll march inland, and be ready when the time comes. Keep up your courage! We will fight when we are ready!"

His voice rose into a cry. The troops listened, but still demanded to fight.

"Now! Fight now!" they bellowed back at him.

"Victory must be certain when we fight. The victims of the Alamo and the men who were murdered at Goliad cry out for vengeance. We can't let them down by fighting too soon. We must retreat and choose the place for our victory. We must not make one mistake."

The men were dirty, tired, sick, and wet. Despite their condition, they roared at him.

"Find the Mexicans! Fight them now!"

I watched Sam stand alone in the spreading gloom. He pitted his will against the men and ordered them to find cover from a gathering thunderstorm.

"I have a mob, not an army," he whispered to me later. From then on he gave orders without explanation. He talked to me in private, and no one else knew his plans.

The next day he called us dogs to his shelter under an oak tree. At his side stood a wiry young man wearing doeskin pants, a flannel shirt, and moccasins. A red cloth fit snuggly around his head.

"This is Beaver. He is part Cherokee and speaks the language well." Sam picked up a stick, got out his knife and whittled as fast as he talked.

"I've just heard Chief Jim Jolly is in Texas now. I've asked Beaver to find him and ask him to stop his braves and others from attacking the refugees. We can't fight Indians and Mexicans. We need his help." He dropped the stick and put his knife in his pocket as he reached to pet us.

"I want all of you, Liberty, Justice, and F'rall, to go with Beaver. The chief remembers you, Liberty, and will listen to you. It's urgent that you start right away. Can I depend on you to take care of Beaver and see that he finds the chief?"

F'rall mumbled. Justice and I looked Sam in the eye and then each gave him a paw. He stroked us, and thanked F'rall for speaking for all of us.

"Take care of each other," he said as he shook Beaver's hand.

"You'll find these dogs are courageous creatures, and will strike terror into the heart of an enemy. They will attack fearlessly when danger threatens. Treat them well!"

I hoped we wouldn't have to attack anyone, but we were willing to fight for Sam.

-8-
The Plot Curdles

Beaver rode a pinto, the fastest horse I ever tried to outrun. We needed to make good speed, so we followed wherever he led us.

The worst part was that we had a silent trip. With Sam we always knew what he expected of us. He talked all the time. Beaver went about his business, ignoring us. We had to guess what he would do next. He never spoke.

The first few days we traveled through rolling country covered with woods. We passed through an occasional meadow and heavy woods along the banks of the Guadalupe River. We ate turkey and squirrels mostly, and the three of us slept curled close together in the hollows of an uprooted tree. Sometimes we slept beside the fire when Beaver took time to gather twigs.

Each day we jogged steadily along. Deer ranged near us, but we could only watch the soft-eyed creatures drink and graze. We had no time to chase them.

One afternoon we came upon two large piles of antelope dung. I jumped in and rolled back and forth. F'rall barked and flung himself about on the other pad. Justice stood nearby watching us. We soon introduced him to this great pleasure. Once he tried it, he liked it as much as we did.

We didn't get to stay nearly long enough. Beaver never stopped for important things, and our tumbling around in the dung made him furious. He rode faster through the trees, until it was hard even for me to keep up with him.

He didn't like us any better that night. He failed to toss us scraps after he ate, and insisted we sleep six trees away from him that night and the next.

During the day, he tried many tricks to lose us. Once he and his horse swam downstream in a river for hours. When he finally rode out splashing and grinning, his grin turned to grunts. He turned away and slapped his knee, because we were sitting on the bank waiting for him. He hadn't seen us cross the river.

I wished Sam had given us a friendlier traveling companion, but since he knew where to go we followed like soldiers.

One morning as we trotted along a deer trail, I had an edgy sense of being watched. I didn't see anything, but it felt as if a big cat was near. It moved somewhere behind us without making a sound, and came closer in the afternoon. I ran beside Beaver's foot, whining softly to warn him. He ignored me.

Every nerve in my body felt wary and suspicious. We needed to find out what was following us. Justice and F'rall ran with me, ears pricked and eyes alert. A porcupine scrambled noisily down a tree trunk and disappeared into the brush. A squirrel flew across the trail in a flash toward a high branch. Two birds squawked and wings fluttered as they swiftly vanished from sight.

The horse pranced about, bucked again and again until Beaver gave him his head to race ahead.

We were all moving at top speed when a shot rang out, followed by a loud thump. Something heavy hit the ground not far behind us.

Soon another shot, too close to my ears, filled the air. I jumped, bumping into Justice. Before landing on top of him, I saw that the horse was shot. The animal swerved and then dropped to the ground, trapping Beaver's leg in the fall.

-9-
Disaster Strikes

My first thought was to run for cover when I heard that shot, but then I saw poor Beaver. He was pinned under the dead horse, trying to pull his leg out from under it. He needed help.

Ignoring the danger, I ran to him and started digging beside his leg as fast as my paws could fling away the dirt. Justice joined me to dig on the other side. Before long we had made a place big enough for him to pull his leg out. He used both hands and eased it an inch at a time. Finally it was free, but the shape of his leg looked different.

Beaver's face twisted in pain as he edged himself slowly away from us. He used one arm to drag his body in the dirt and the other to hold his leg. He leaned against a tree, groaning, his eyes closed and tears rolling down his cheeks.

"Go," he whispered to us. "Get away while you can. My leg is broken!"

I had a better idea. There was a hollow on the other side of the tree nearly filled with damp, rotting leaves. Justice and I pushed the leaves aside and nudged Beaver into the hollow. F'rall helped us cover him with leaves.

Then the three of us rolled around in the dirt to rub out our tracks before we found our own hiding places.

None of us moved. There were sounds of men pushing through the undergrowth. They were calling to each other, and they were not speaking English. We waited, not daring to touch a twig or stir a leaf.

It seemed as if we were there for hours, almost afraid to breathe, when two soldiers broke through the clearing with guns held ready to fire.

They spoke softly to each other when they saw the horse. They crept in and out of the trees without finding Beaver's hollow.

At one point one of them stood with his back close to me. He pulled a wild onion up near his boot and ate it. The smell nearly made me sneeze before he dropped the stem and sauntered back to his buddy.

Then they tried to steal the fallen horse's bridle. They had trouble doing it, but finally one of them managed to yank the bridle out from under the dead animal. One of the men flipped it over his shoulder and walked off through the woods.

They talked steadily, so when their voices

faded, we knew it was safe to come out of hiding.

We checked on Beaver, carefully scooping the leaves away from his body. He shook his head and flipped the last small twig and the leaves from his ear. He pointed to a smooth branch a few feet away. I picked it up in my mouth and dropped it by his leg. Then he motioned for me to bring him a soft vine from a nearby tree. I did, and Justice pulled more of the vine and dropped it beside mine.

Beaver spent a long time placing his leg just right. Then he wrapped the vine around the tree limb and his leg several times to hold it in place. He fell back against the tree trunk, exhausted and pale.

"Those were Mexican soldiers," he whispered. "There must be others lurking around. Look that way. Maybe you'll see more of them, but move slowly."

We crept around in the direction of his

nod, but saw nothing. The search went on in all directions before we came back and plopped down beside him.

"Where's F'rall?" he asked.

Justice and I raced to our hiding place. F'rall was not there. We raced back and forth through the trees, finding only his scent and the route he had taken. I hurried back to Beaver wondering why F'rall had left and where he had gone. I wanted to follow him, but Beaver was hurt. We needed to stay and protect him.

-10-
F'rall Saves the Day

Justice and I scouted for soldiers and searched for food. We didn't see a sign of the men. The only live creature we found was a mouse, which ran into a thick bush and disappeared before we reached it.

Beaver was lucky. He had a piece of jerky in his pocket and water in the canteen he wore around his waist.

He was afraid to build a fire. Some soldiers might be near enough to see it or smell it. He decided we should stay put for the night so he could rest his leg. He said he would come up with a plan tomorrow.

We drank plenty of water, but we didn't find any food. Justice was hungrier than I was—he caught a frog and ate it. I chewed on some of the plants on the edge of a small pond, but I didn't swallow them. They had a bitter taste. The frogs were safe from me.

Beaver was shaking all over and his teeth were chattering when we got back. He called us to his side, "I'm cold. Come over here!"

So the three of us lay down side by side, even though it was still light. We pushed against him until he relaxed. Then we all dozed for a while. It felt good to rest, but my eyes stayed open most of the time.

A curious squirrel peered at us from a nearby tree. I kept my eye on him. Food at last, I thought, but it scurried up the tree out of sight before I could move. I heard the soft flutter of wings as a sparrow landed on a branch above my head. He tilted his head as he called to his mate to come join him.

Beaver smelled like rotting leaves and made a hissing sound when he breathed. There was also a rabbit smell somewhere near that needed to be checked on.

A sudden sound of footsteps in leaves startled the bird and it flew away. I sprang up, teeth bared, eyes narrowed, hackles raised, and tail thrust outward. There was no time to hide Beaver. Justice snarled beside me, every hair on his back and ruff erect. The footsteps got closer. We waited.

We were poised to pounce on the enemy when F'rall ran from the brush and jumped on us. He started licking my face and wagging his tail. He laid his ears flat, slanted his eyes back until they almost disappeared, then drew his lips back over his teeth in a grin as a man came into view. I knew that face.

The man held his gun ready to fire until

he saw me. Beaver groaned at the sight of the stranger, and tried to slide away.

"You're hurt, man! So you're why F'rall insisted on bringing me here." He put his gun down at once and knelt beside Beaver's injured leg.

"It's broken right here below my knee. I tried to push the break together . . ." Beaver's face was even paler and his mouth twitched.

The man's broad hands felt along the leg slowly and carefully several times before he spoke. "Feels like you did it right. But we need to get you up off the damp ground." He gathered broken branches and covered them with dry leaves.

"I'm Henry Black," he said as he helped Beaver ease himself onto the twig bed. "The dogs came to our cabin with Sam Houston once. We'll always be friends."

He moved the broken leg an inch at a

time, and piled more leaves under it until Beaver stopped him.

"It feels better now. Thanks. How'd you find me?"

"Mexican soldiers rushed our cabin this afternoon. They scared us, but they didn't hurt me or my wife Nellie." He crossed himself, bowed his head and closed his eyes for a second.

"They stole our only horse, a cow, all the chickens they could catch, and a pig. Somehow our goats got away from them.

"As soon as the soldiers left, I took the goat cart and set out to look for them. One of our pigs should be out there, also. I hoped to find 'em before dark." Henry squatted close to Beaver, felt the break in his leg again, took off his hat and wiped his forehead with the back of his hand.

"F'rall came along just as I spotted one of the goats. He helped me catch her, then led me to you. In my hurry to follow F'rall, I tied her to the cart and left it halfway between here and our cabin. I'll go get it and take you home to Nellie's good care." He stood up, slapped his hat against his thigh and plopped it back on his head.

"F'rall, come with me. It might be dark before we get back. I'll need you to help me find them again."

Henry rubbed behind my ears before he left. I slobbered on his hand to show my gratitude and then went over and stretched out beside Beaver. Justice went off with them for a while, but he soon came back and flopped down beside me. Beaver sighed, closed his eyes, and went to sleep.

-11-
We Take the News to Sam

Beaver called out in pain twice in his sleep. He also mumbled Cherokee words and sobbed deeply. He hurt worse than he admitted. We pushed our bodies against him for comfort, hoping Henry and F'rall would be there soon with the cart. But before long Justice and I both drifted off to sleep. It had been a hard day.

I don't know how long we slept. Voices woke me. Justice's head went up, his ears bent to the sound. A group of men were softly speaking Spanish a few trees away. It sounded as if Mexican soldiers were making camp. Soon I smelled wood burning.

Beaver opened his eyes and motioned for us to be still. It was nearly dark, but the soldiers could see us if they came this way. Our only hope was silence. The waiting seemed endless.

It became even harder not to move a muscle when they put food on to cook. Tantalizing smells of roasting chicken soon filled the air. I closed my eyes and tried not to remember how it felt and tasted to bite into a bird cooked over a fire. My insides ached, and I turned my nose toward the fire light in spite of myself. To smell food, with no hope of eating it, was torture.

Beaver and Justice stared at the trees in front of them. Beaver's tongue rolled around his lips. Justice rested his head on his paws and swallowed several times.

I felt proud to know that the best smells in

the world could never force this brave man or us dogs into careless action.

While the meat cooked, the soldiers sang one sad ballad after another. Far off in the woods a coyote choir sounded its own lament, and I bit my tongue so I wouldn't be tempted to join.

Suddenly a man on horseback rode out of the dark. He came close to us as he moved toward the soldiers. The singing stopped. Angry shouts filled the air, followed by quick movements and heavy boots running in the brush. The fire turned to heavy smoke. Someone had smothered it with damp dirt.

In no time the smoke disappeared and they all marched off into the woods. The man on horsback shouted angrily after them.

We waited, not daring to move until the men were gone.

My first thought was to rush to where the fire had been and see if they had left any food. Before I could, F'rall came running out of the woods. Henry soon appeared behind him.

"We've been hiding," Henry whispered. "We were afraid the Mexicans would find all of us if we came near. I hope they don't find the cart and take it with them." Henry knelt beside Beaver and asked him, "Beaver, did you hear them say why they left in such a hurry?"

"Yes," he raised himself slowly on one elbow and took a drink from his canteen before going on, "I need to get back right away. The officer on horseback told the others that a spy had found Houston and the Texans. The Mexican Army is moving toward them at full speed. They burned Harrisburg, where the Texas government had fled, as well as every other town they passed. I need to get word to General Houston." His voice trembled. He moved his leg and cried out in pain.

"You can't. Not with that leg." Henry patted his shoulder. "But Liberty, Justice, and F'rall can take a message to him. They can get back to him faster than you could, even if you were able to ride the fastest mount."

"Yes, they can do that!" Beaver pulled the red cloth from his head. "We can pin a message in this and tie it around Liberty's neck. But what can we write on?"

Henry thrust his hands in his pocket and drew them out to show he had nothing.

Beaver shook his head and bit his lip.

I danced and yammered and rolled around in the leaves. I was filled with joy and excitement thinking I might help Sam win the war. If only I could have talked! "We have paper at the cabin, but by the time we pull you there in the cart, too much time will be lost," Henry scratched his chin. "I'll go look around where the soldiers camped. Maybe they left something."

We followed him through the trees. A sliver of a moon shone in the west. It wasn't bright enough to see much, but we could smell the fire. The three of us searched every rock and inch of dirt around the dying fire until our paws burned. We learned fast that they had taken everything with them.

Henry talked to himself as he poked around. Soon he came back to the fire bed, pushing the charred wood with the toe of his boot.

"Charcoal and tree bark will have to do," he said as he juggled a piece of hot wood. He finally dropped it and picked it up again. It was covered with dirt. He felt the bark of several trees as we walked along.

Beaver greeted us with his knife pointing to a slender poplar tree a few feet away. "I think that one is smooth enough. Try it."

Henry cut the bark in several places and peeled it back until he had a piece the size of a note. By then the charred wood was cool enough to hold, and he wrote the message on a stump.

Beaver took a safety pin from inside his waist. "This helped keep my pants up. Guess I won't be needing it for a while."

Henry pinned the note inside the cloth and then tied it around my neck. I felt proud to be in charge of such an important mission.

"Take this to Sam as fast as you can, Liberty. That's a good dog. Go to Sam!"

"Watch out for Mexican soldiers! Good luck!" Beaver shouted.

As soon as the note was secure, we were on our way. I heard Henry speak as we raced away through the trees, "I'll go get the cart now and take you home, Beaver."

We had a long trip ahead of us, but I knew nothing must stop us from taking the news to Sam.

-12-
Good Judgement Pays Off

We raced along through the trees. The woods were silent and still. Men must have come this way not long ago and frightened the creatures away. It's a good thing we stayed alert, for soon we heard heavy movement through the brush.

We walked lightly and slowly. The movement stopped, and we heard voices calling back and forth to each other. An angry shout stopped the talking. All was quiet, but we came close enough to see that the Mexican Army was marching ahead of us.

We crept around the first of them, careful

not to move a twig. One look-out soldier on the edge of camp came too near us. We had to slide and wiggle along on our bellies until we were far away from him. The rest of them had stopped to rest, so we had plenty of time to find the long way around them and then hurry on our way again.

But we soon came upon more Mexican soldiers. All night long we managed to pass safely around the camped troops without any of them knowing we were there. But we lost precious time.

Then Justice and F'rall wasted more time by marking trees. I stopped and told them that if they intended to mark every tree we passed, then they should just stay there and do it. I said that I'd take the message to Sam. They both hung their heads. They didn't mark any more trees that night.

When dawn came, we hoped the threat was behind us. We stopped at a small stream to drink, and then hid in a hollow log for a much needed nap.

I dreamed of finding a large bowl of chicken scraps in gravy like the one Nellie Black had fixed us. I was putting my face to the bowl to start eating when a gunshot woke me.

I wiggled out from the log when I heard the blast. Justice and F'rall followed close behind me. We sat low in the leaves and brush, waiting.

We didn't see or hear anything for a long time. Then another shot rang out in the distance. Perhaps the Mexican soldiers were hunting. We needed to get out of their way.

We kept a good pace all morning with no interruptions, stopping for water twice and nearly cornering a wild pig. Sam had said the Texans called them javelinas. It got away from us and ran into a bog. We searched, but never found it or anything else to ease the pain in our empty bellies.

Surely we would find food soon, I thought. My trot turned to a slow walk as we made our way through desolate country. We had not seen a human all day or found anything we could eat. Constant hunger left me weary and aching. Even a frog might tempt my famished insides. But we didn't have to settle for frogs. A faint whiff of wood smoke ahead sent us dashing off in that direction. We soon came upon a small cabin and a smokehouse. The buildings stood on the edge of a newly plowed field. I could see a small stream through the bushes on the other side. There were no farm animals about.

Approaching cautiously, we walked up on the porch of the cabin and scratched at the door. No one came to greet us. I reached a ledge with my front paws and looked through a window. No one was home.

Next we clawed and pushed on the door of

the smokehouse. It held fast, and there were no windows.

The shack was supported on each corner by smooth river rocks. F'rall crouched down and crawled underneath. I could hear his body dragging along in the small space. There were scuffling sounds and the crash of a board breaking. F'rall had pulled himself inside. He moved around and started jumping at the door. With a strong leap, he pushed it open and fell out on the ground holding a slab of bacon in his mouth. He dropped it in front of me. The salty smell nearly drove me crazy.

The three of us tore at it and gulped it down until nothing was left but a few bits of fat in the dust.

We all went inside the shack searching for more food. When we were certain it was empty, we went to drink from the stream. We drank our fill and rested by the bank.

Every hour brought us closer to Sam. The food gave us a needed boost of energy for the run through the deserted country. The closest we saw to a living thing was an area covered with empty snake skins.

But we had company in the sky. Two mockingbirds seemed bent on making the journey with us. Their songs cheered me on, and I missed them when they flew away. It was nearly dark when we stopped to rest again.

This time we shared a large mesquite tree for the night. It was near the big river where Beaver had tried to lose us that day. A rabbit jumped out as I edged my way under a branch and sank to the ground. I was too tired to chase it. Justice plopped down beside me. F'rall ran after it, but was too slow. All I wanted was to rest my weary body.

Thunder woke me sometime before dawn. I couldn't see the clouds gathering, but I could sense them. It would be best to swim across that river before the storm started, I thought.

I pulled myself up and stretched. Justice and F'rall stood beside me at the water's edge. We looked, listened, and waited. Lightning flashed all over the sky. We stood poised, ready to jump in and swim to the opposite shore. My chest felt tight, and something told me to wait to cross the river. But there was no time to waste. I ignored my hunch.

-13-
Disaster Strikes Again

We held our stance there, ready to jump into the river. Then a flash of lightning and a blast of thunder sent us tumbling back under the bush. We barely missed being pelted by hail as large as pigeon eggs. We huddled close to the ground. Luckily, it stopped soon after it started.

We ventured out to witness the ground covered by lumps of ice. F'rall ate one hailstone after another. He thought they were delicious. Perhaps he didn't know they were nothing more than solid water. He enjoyed each mouthful, throwing his head around. He dropped some on the ground, then scooped them up again with his tongue. I hated to take him away from his fun.

I watched the river. Soon there were no more flashes of light or rumbling thunder, except in the distance. The storm had moved swiftly on its way. It seemed to be a good time to turn F'rall away from his hailstones and start our race back to Sam. At that moment Justice took off after a rabbit.

It was light in the east when he returned. His tail hung between his legs and his eyes were downcast. He had no rabbit.

By then F'rall was bored with the hailstones. The three of us stood on the bank. When it seemed right, we took a few careful steps into the river. We started out cautiously. Justice plopped in first and we followed.

We were all in the water paddling toward the opposite shore. I looked up to see a wall of water roaring down the river toward us. I'd seen a flash flood with Sam once, but I'd never actually *been* in one before. That time we had waited an entire day before we dared cross that river. Why hadn't we waited this time? The thought pounded in my head.

We all sensed the danger at once and swam as fast as our legs would move us. We had nearly reached the bank when a great curling wave surged over us. It carried small trees, torn branches, parts of the river bank, and whirling logs.

I was pulled deep into the churning water. I emerged choking and breathless to see a log hit F'rall in the head.

The next time I saw him he was limp and halfway under water. He was caught in the debris that raged down the river.

I swam toward him with all my strength. The sun was coming up, so I could see where I was going.

Justice was just pulling himself onto land

when I spotted him. He barked for help, then jumped back in immediately to save our drowning pup.

Just as we were nearly in reach, the log spun around and sent him into a whirling surge down the river. He disappeared from sight.

Justice and I were both strong swimmers, but the current was stronger. We finally managed to pull out of the foaming deluge and stand on firm ground.

We had barely taken a deep breath before we had to race further down the riverbank. We searched the chaos of the wild churning river for any sign of him.

At one point Justice almost fell in. He jumped away just in time. Part of the riverbank was sucked into the raging river. I nearly slipped back in twice, but we couldn't let anything slow us down. We had to save F'rall.

-14-

We Save F'rall

It seemed like we ran beside that river forever, with no sign of F'rall anywhere. I was out of breath, covered with mud, and frantic. What if the river carried him away, and I never found him? The thought chilled me.

Suddenly I stopped to stare at a pile of assorted branches and debris. Something else was caught there. Did I see a dog's head?

I wasn't sure until I plunged in near it and saw that it really was F'rall.

I grabbed his neck in my teeth, the way I carried him as a puppy, and swam toward land. Justice had come in with me, and now shoved and pushed the limp body from behind.

I backed onto the shore. Together we pulled and pushed until we had him stretched out on the ground with his head down.

Green liquid dribbled from his mouth. Then he shook. He suddenly choked and struggled for breath, and a gush of water poured out of him. Then he lay relaxed. I bent close. He was breathing! He was alive! We had gotten to him in time.

I ran around him barking and nudging him all over with my nose. Nothing woke him, but he was alive. With great relief I pushed my body against him for comfort, hoping he would open his eyes soon.

We spent most of the morning by the bank of the river. F'rall woke once, stumbled about, and more water gushed from his mouth. After that he sighed, plopped down, and went back to sleep. We rested with him in peace after the violence of the morning. The sun dried us. Our bellies gave hungry rumbles, but this morning we needed rest more than food.

After a while F'rall got up, stretched, ambled around, and soon became frisky and eager to move along.

Justice yawned, scratched his ear, and pulled himself up. Then he froze with one leg in the air, his ears perked. In less than a second he dashed away. I sprang after him but I lost him. I returned to wait with F'rall.

The wait was not long. He came back carrying a turkey, the best meal we'd had in days. Besides a few feathers on the grass and bushes, after we finished nothing was left but bones, a beak, a comb, and feet.

We continued our journey in high spirits. At first we stopped often for F'rall to rest, but soon he was able to keep up with us as if nothing had happened.

Sometimes we ran on deer trails that made green tunnels in the trees. When the trees thinned out, we cut straight through the brush and grass even faster.

Every day and every hour brought us closer to Sam. When the others stopped to chase a rabbit, I went on without them. They soon followed. I was afraid if we wasted any time, our news might arrive too late to help the Texans.

At dusk Justice found the biggest rabbit I had ever seen. We shared it to keep up our strength, and we made even better time after we ate it.

That night we slept curled closely together in a hollow under an old, spreading oak tree, near a small stream. Long before dawn broke, we started again.

The closer we got, the faster we traveled. I knew it wouldn't be long, and the excitement of being with Sam again was almost more than I could stand to imagine.

We often passed deer. We chased them for the fun of it, but I didn't allow much wandering from our chosen path.

The biggest temptation was fresh antelope dung. It was too hard to pass it by without rolling in it, so we all took a quick roll. What a comfort to have that fine smell with us for the rest of the day.

-15-
Sam Gets Ready for War

We found Sam that night. He had made camp in a grove of live oak trees on a bluff near the San Jacinto River. Sam was talking to two captains by a campfire. His back turned when we bounded out of the darkness and into the ring of firelight. We all rushed at him at once and nearly pushed him into the fire. He turned and looked at us as if we were ghosts.

"What are you doing here?" he said.

I nearly went out of my mind with excitement, covering his hands with frantic licking, as he stroked and hugged us and finally

squatted to have his face licked by three tongues at once.

"Hold it!" he shouted, petting each of us in turn.

Then he untied the knot and lifted the red cloth from around my neck. He unpinned it and spread it out on the ground, studying it in the light of the fire. He turned it around and motioned for the captains to help him.

They both gave their interpretation of what was written on the bark. Sam picked it up and read slowly, often adding his own words.

"Prepare. Santa Anna knows where you are and is marching his army of over 1,000 men toward you. He burned Harrisburg and all the other towns he passed. Our government got away. Beaver will stay with us until his broken leg heals. God bless you, Henry Black."

"Thank you for bringing this so quickly,

Liberty. Now we know what to expect. Bring food for these brave dogs, and then let them rest. They deserve the best we have. They may have saved us all."

The next morning Sam had the troops up maneuvering before dawn. They seemed fit and ready, but they had no practice shooting. Gun powder was too precious. Justice, F'rall, and I did what we did best—we watched and rested and hoped the Mexicans were still behind us trying to cross the river.

But two days later, hiding behind a rise of ground and Spanish moss, we dogs watched the Mexican Army march across the plains toward us.

On each side of the grove of oak trees where we camped stood a cannon. Sam called those guns the Twin Sisters.

"Those sisters were sent to us from the good people of Cincinnati, Ohio," Sam told us. He pointed to a pile of broken horseshoes beside each cannon. "They will be the ammunition. When the Mexicans fire their rifles, the Twin Sisters will return horseshoes." Sam was the kind of guy who'd slap his leg and laugh in spite of his worries and haggard face. He didn't look as if he'd slept since we left.

Santa Anna marched his troops nearby, and set up camp between marshes and a boggy bayou.

"That is just where I hoped he would camp. That's Santa Anna's big mistake." Sam hooted when he saw them make camp. He ordered all the bridges across the river destroyed.

"The only way the Mexicans can escape is through the marshes or the road toward Harrisburg," Sam told us. "If they do, we will stop them. It's now or never!"

The Texans could see the retreat was over.

"Let's start now," they begged. "Let's shoot it out once and for all."

Sam held them back.

"I'm waiting for Santa Anna to make another mistake," he told me. "Keep watching. He will. "

When night came, we could see the Mexicans' campfires. We were camped so close to them that it was easy for us dogs to see and hear what was happening.

Sam had guessed right. His Spanish-speaking spy told him the Mexicans were discussing how they would wipe Sam Houston and his troops from the earth with little effort in the morning.

The Texans settled in for a much needed good night's sleep.

"I slept well for the first time in weeks," Sam said the next morning as he watched the troops prepare for the fight.

"Hold your fire," Sam told them. "Our eight hundred angry men will be all the strength we need. Do you want to fight?" A shout went up, and Sam answered them, "Very well. Eat some food. Get some rest. I will lead you into a fight, and if you whip them, every one of you will be a captain."

Sam waited all morning for the Mexicans to start the war, but Santa Anna didn't attack. The spy said he was waiting for more troops to arrive to help him destroy the Texans.

At midday Sam heard that the Mexicans ate a hearty meal of beef they had stolen from a nearby farm. Then they settled in for their usual siesta. Even Santa Anna was napping in his tent.

Sam acted fast. Because of the wet weather, he ordered the troops to take the old ammunition out of their guns and put in fresh. He gave us dogs orders to stay safely behind the lines.

We stayed out of Sam's way so he wouldn't worry, but we had our own battle plans.

Nothing could keep us from helping. We knew what to do.

Sam, on his white stallion Saracen, rode up and down the lines muttering, "Hold your fire. Hold your fire. The time is near. Move slowly and quietly, and hold your fire!"

Sam and Saracen were an impressive sight arranging the troops in battle order. The fife and drum corps prepared to strike up a tune. It was time to begin. "It's now or never!" Sam told his aides.

-16-
Sam Wins the War

"Now!" Sam gave the signal. Three taps on a drum told the troops to get ready. The Twin Sisters were moved and prepared to fire. Sam rode back and forth on his white stallion, giving orders.

The fife and drum corps struck up a tune called, "Will you Come to the Bower I Have Shaded for You?" It was the only song they knew—a silly love song I hated. I put my paws over my ears and moaned. F'rall held his head back and howled in protest. Like me, he couldn't stand to hear it one more time. I still wonder why they didn't learn a marching song.

In perfect battle order, the troops advanced. They looked better than they had ever looked when they practiced. Sam must have felt proud.

I'd listened to the soldiers complaining all day. They were saying: "I'm tired of waiting. Yes, we've waited long enough. Let's take 'em, now. What's keeping Old Sam? I'm ready. Let's fight. I'd rather fight than wait!"

The waiting was over. This was it!

Soon cries of, "Remember the Alamo! Remember Goliad! Now or never!" overpowered that boring love song.

We were close to the line when a sudden bugle blast came from the Mexicans' camp.

Musket fire rang out. As we raced toward them, I saw some Mexicans waking up from their afternoon siesta. Some were half-dressed and in great confusion. Their guns had been stacked together. The men fell over each other trying to reach their guns. They were surprised that we Texans were brave enough to charge an army twice our size.

Fire rang out as the Mexicans and Texans met. The battle was on.

There was a loud bang. I heard a soldier shout that one of the Twin Sisters had blasted one of the Mexicans' cannons.

Our troops charged the Mexican barricades. They jumped over them, shooting and cutting their way through their defenses.

The fire from the Texas rifles was thick around us. I watched many Mexicans throw down their guns and run away. Texas soldiers were all over the enemy.

"Take prisoners! Don't let 'em get away," a captain shouted.

"Remember the Alamo! Remember the Alamo! Remember Goliad!" the troops screamed as they attacked.

Justice, F'rall, and I followed our own battle plan. It worked well because no one expected it. Each of us charged a Mexican soldier at gun level, knocking him and his weapon to the ground. Then we stood on top of him with our mouth on his neck, until a Texan came along to take him prisoner. Sometimes in his hurry to get away, the Mexican soldier would trip over us. Then we would hold him until he could be captured.

At one point I thought I was going to die. A Mexican soldier had his gun pointed at me, ready to fire. Justice sprang out of nowhere onto the enemy's back. The man fell forward, and Justice held his neck in his mouth. I noticed Justice's paw was bleeding, but that didn't stop him. He was gone before I could thank him.

F'rall was good at dashing in front of the fleeing enemy. He tripped two or three Mexican soldiers at once. I helped him hold them until our men came.

I tried to stay near Sam when I wasn't

holding a Mexican. Just when I thought we were together again, he was gone. I saw Saracen shot down. Sam jumped on another horse nearby. The next time I saw him he was on a third horse leading a charge. I noticed that blood covered his boot.

There was no time to think about how to help him. With chaos everywhere, we kept on fighting the best we could. I tried to make myself believe Sam's wound wasn't serious.

Soon a bugle blasted a call. I didn't understand what it meant, but the firing stopped. Our troops were shouting and screaming to each other. It took a while for us to learn what had happened. The noise was terrible. We couldn't make out the words until the soldier shouted and chanted together: "We did it! We took the Mexicans! They surrendered! We won! We won! The battle is over! Mexicans surrendered! Texas is free! Texas is independent! Hail the Lone Star Republic!"

We watched the Mexican soldiers throw down their guns and hold their hands in the air. Our troops, singing and shouting, rounded up the prisoners.

Justice, F'rall, and I joined the celebration. Later I saw that Justice's paw wasn't seriously injured. We three found a quiet spot under a mulberry tree and took a much needed nap. As I dozed off, someone shouted that the battle had lasted eighteen minutes.

-17-
Sam Survives

Justice and F'rall helped me search the battlefield for Sam. It was a mess. Our soldiers were hard at work rounding up prisoners, but Sam was not with them. I thought about his bloody boot. I hoped he would be okay. We looked among the prisoners and the wounded, but couldn't find Sam.

Sam Houston lived a charmed life. He had told me about a battle where he fought beside Andrew Jackson long ago. In that battle he was wounded with a barbed arrow in the thigh and two slugs in the shoulder. The men had left him for dead. Yet, he lived to tell about it.

Another time he fought a duel and came out healthy and laughing. I saw him fight other men many times, but he was never seriously hurt. Whatever happened he always said, "I can take it." I knew he could take anything, but where had he gone?

Finally we found our victorious general sitting under a tree. He reached out to us and ran his fingers lightly over my ears and back. I licked his face. I flopped down next to him while he greeted Justice and F'rall.

A surgeon was trying to dig out bits of metal from his right ankle. A Mexican musket ball had shattered it. His face showed that his wound gave him horrible pain. It didn't keep him from sitting calmly to write news of their victory at San Jacinto to President Andrew Jackson.

Sam finished the letter and sent it with a

messenger. He then braided some magnolia leaves and wildflowers to make a garland for his new lady love, Miss Anna. He gave it to a soldier with a note: "These are laurels I send to you from the battlefield of San Jacinto. Thine. Houston."

I was no help to Sam when it came to his love life. I never stopped wondering how he could be in all that pain and still make a garland. But that was Sam. He was a genius.

Sam turned to us and said, "I wonder how the battle would have ended if the Mexican Army had surprised us—if you hadn't brought news that they were nearly upon us. You are heroes, all three of you. The people of Texas will always be indebted to you. Such bravè dogs!" Sam petted us again as he leaned back against the tree and closed his eyes.

There was great rejoicing in the camp. The men celebrated and sang every song they knew. Some made up tales of bravery they would tell their families when they got home.

There was one sad note. Santa Anna was not among the prisoners. He had sneaked off somewhere, and no one had found him.

Sam pulled Justice close to his side. "Remember who killed your master at the Alamo? Go find him! You can do it," he whispered into Justice's ear.

F'rall and I rushed up, yammering and whining to be taken along.

"No, Liberty, you two wait here. This is something he needs to do alone. He has waited a long time to avenge Bowie. Let him go!"

Justice bowed his head to me and made a dash. I'd never seen him move so fast. Sam laughed. He knew Justice would find Santa Anna, and so did I. After all, Justice would never forget what happened at the Alamo. He needed to find his master's killer, or would die trying. Sam, F'rall, and I watched him go. We could do nothing but wait.

-18-
Justice Gets Revenge

I expected a long wait. I knew Justice would never return without Santa Anna. Santa Anna could have been in Mexico by now to rally another army. Justice was the kind of a dog who would never stop searching. Perhaps I'd never see him again. I wished Sam would have let me go with him.

Sam seemed to ignore the pain from his shattered ankle, but his face was ashen. His hand shook when he wrote, yet he never stopped giving orders nor did he complain about his wound.

The captured Mexican soldiers denied

they were at the Alamo. Their words didn't fool anyone. F'rall wasn't in sight, but I knew he was on the battlefield herding prisoners.

It was a long day for me. All the excitement didn't stop me from worrying about Justice. Sam looked worse every hour.

Toward evening a strange looking man wearing a blue smock and red shoes raced toward us. Justice chased him, snarling and growling. When the man fell to the ground, Justice was on him in a flash. He stood on top of him, holding the man's neck with his teeth.

"Let him go, Justice!" Sam motioned for his aides to pick up the man and hold him. "This soldier disguised himself hoping to run away. Put him with the other prisoners."

Justice barked frantically, snapping at the man's legs. He finally caught his ankle in his teeth and refused to let go. The man kicked and shouted at him, but Justice held on.

A Mexican prisoner turned around when

he heard the stranger's voice. He called out, "El Presidente!" Others joined him, "El Presidente! El Presidente! "

Santa Anna in silly clothes was at last at Sam's mercy.

"Shoot him! Shoot him! Let me shoot him now!" The cry went up all over the battlefield.

Sam Houston had other plans. "No!" he told them. "Thanks to Justice we can keep Santa Anna as a hostage. With him we can force Mexico to recognize the independence of Texas. He is worth more to us alive than dead"

The Texans nearly went crazy, crying over and over, "No, he needs to die!" They begged Sam to let them have their way. No one could change his mind.

After Santa Anna was taken to a safe place, Sam called us to his side. "How can I thank you enough?" He inched his body around trying to make his leg more comfortable. “The people of Texas and I will always be grateful to the three of you. We are free at last and you played a big part in helping us win that freedom. Now Justice has secured it for us. You must be proclaimed heroes of our cause!” He pulled us closer to him and petted and hugged us in turn.

“You helped us become a republic. Now we will live as your names suggest—with Liberty and Justice F’rall—forever. Word of our great victory went out to all the world this day. Your names will be known far and wide, but I hope you will stay with me always.” Sam had tears in his eyes as he leaned against the tree, exhausted.

-19-
Sam Settles Down

My duties ended that day. Sam Houston was carried off the field and hailed as the "Hero of San Jacinto." He liked that title. It gave him great comfort, but it didn't win over Miss Anna.

Being a hero didn't stop Sam's suffering, either. His leg got worse. He was sent to New Orleans for proper medical treatment on the next boat leaving Indianola.

We dogs were taken to Nacogdoches to wait for him there. It was a shame we were not allowed to go with him. His leg became infected during the trip, and a cold nose in the palm of his hand would have helped him heal.

I heard later that there were hundreds of people at the dock to greet him when his ship landed in New Orleans. When he was carried onto the dock they shouted, "Hail, Hero of San Jacinto." A band played.

Standing with her family, one young lady sighed over Sam, and tears filled her eyes. Her name was Margaret Lea.

He hardly remembered being taken off the ship and rushed to the hospital, but he remembered Margaret. She came often to see him while he was ill. The same doctor who had cared for him after his last battle wounds removed twenty bits of loose bone from his leg.

Sam hovered near death for weeks. Margaret Lea's visits eased his pain, and they became close friends.

He recovered to be elected the first president of the Texas Republic, but doctors told him he would limp the rest of his life.

Margaret Lea become his bride and caretaker. Sometimes I didn't think she did as good a job as I did, but my work was finished.

"I'll build a house for my children and you, my dogs. The people of this country will long remember what you did. You'll go down in history," Sam told us many times. But Sam never had time to write down our good deeds.

We didn't mind. We all enjoyed a happy life at the home he built for Margaret and his children. We had no duties, so we romped and played all day. We helped raise the young Houstons.

It was enough for me to know that for a while I was the best friend of a genius and patriot who became the first president of the Republic of Texas, a United States Senator, and later, the governor of Texas.

The freedom of Texas from Mexico

resulted in Texas, New Mexico, Arizona, Nevada, California, Utah, parts of Colorado, Wyoming, Kansas, and Oklahoma becoming states in the Unites States of America.

I cherish the memory of those days. I wrote this account for my offspring, so they will know and remember that their ancestors helped make it all happen.

The End